Eight short stories, worked on, sweated over, edited and finally put into a book!

The authors of these are the long suffering students of 'Creative Writing for Beginners'.

The course was tutored by me, Sandy Stafford. I have been running writing courses for beginners for some time. I like to finish the course with an Anthology of the student's work and all the students who attended this course have worked very hard to 'kill their darlings' and produce a piece of work they can be proud of.

Published by **A S Publishing**
aspublishing.co.uk

©2014

ISBN 978-0-9929812-3-5

I am John Hurst and I am married to Christine.

We live in the beautiful county of Suffolk and have four children and eight grandchildren. I have always wanted to write but have never been sure if what I wrote would be of interest to others. Perhaps that makes me very similar to the majority of aspiring writers.

Betrayal

Two lights flicker in the lonely cottage on the cliff top. Has Fisherman Jo got company or is this just a gesture of extravagance? The lights can be seen from out at sea even though a slight mist is drifting inland.

Satisfied that all his plans are in place for tonight's escapade with the gang Jo retires to bed with his partner Ellie. Ellie has other ideas. All his warm advances are coldly and persistently rejected. Usually Ellie is as eager for their love making as Jo is.

"What's the matter with you woman?" he grumbles.

"Nuffin'."

Frustrated Jo rolls onto his back and tries to sleep but cannot. Ellie pretends to sleep but her emotions are very different. She has been thinking a lot and can forgive his drinking, his swearing and brawling but not this. Ellie feels deeply hurt and betrayed by Jo's actions and one of the ways to get even is to curtail his conjugal rights. She wonders for how long though as this man stirs passions within her that no other man has ever done. Blast him, she wishes she did not love him so much. The village gossip that has filtered through to her is that Jo has been bedding that trollop Maggie from the River Barge Inn. What has she got that Ellie does not give Jo?

***

Jo listens for Ellie's breathing and decides she is asleep, he creeps from under the covers and pads quietly downstairs. Jo slips on his leather boots and the jacket that is hanging on the hook on the front door. Stuffs his pistols into his belt and very quietly lets himself out. His black shaggy hound Shuck is at his heels. Ellie hears the front door catch click.

"I hope you're not off to see that Maggie?" Ellie rants to herself. "If you are you'll regret it Jo me boyee. There's going to be only one woman

3

in your life and that's me." She is soon out of bed, slinging a shawl around her shoulders and following. This jealousy is driving her insane.

Jo looks at Shuck walking along beside him. A tiny smile plays on his lips as he recalls how he first got Shuck. One morning, three years ago, while walking the shingle shore line on his way to check his boat he spied a black bundle, which turned out to be a puppy. Thinking it had been drowned he picked it up; it felt cold but was breathing. Stuffing it under his jacket, he hurried back to the cottage. Ellie and Jo nursed it back to health. They grew to love this little creature as if it were one of their own. Jo felt they should call him 'Lucky' or 'Luck' for short but one of his drinking friends, while under the influence, kept calling him, 'Sh-Shuck' and that is what he became. The dog grew into a colossal hound. Jet black with a glossy, shaggy long coat. Completely devoted to Jo and Ellie and their friends. Unfortunately, to those outside this close-knit unit Shuck is often the most terrifying and fearsome of beasts. His growl starts low and hardly audible. Is then deep, menacing and threatening, ending in a fang bared snarl. His eyes flash with a demonic malevolence and the hackles on the back of his neck rise. If any unwanted guest does not retreat at this stage, Shuck emits a hideous howl and attacks. Jo and Ellie feel quite secure in their remote cottage.

The sea path has shrubbery on either side and leads to a crossroads, so there is plenty of cover for Ellie to follow unseen. Jo reaches the crossroads but instead of turning towards the cove. There is but one dwelling down this path. Surely, Jo cannot be carrying on with the boat builder's wife as well?

"You swine!" Ellie fumes to herself.

The boat builder's house comes into view but Jo walks straight past and carries on towards the cove. Most of the sea mist has cleared, as the moon has risen, apart from a think blanket hanging above the water. Jo does not like this. A dark night would have been better. Two horses and carts stand still, waiting. Just the soft clink of the bridle and horse brasses now and then.

Out of the mist glides a long rowing boat. Immediately a gang of men, including Jo, appears on the shore to beach the boat, which is heavily laden with casks and crates. Jo is directing operations. Ellie crouches, fascinated. Everyone knows what they are doing and no word is spoken -----directions are by hand signals. They work quickly and one horse and cart is soon on its way up the creek and the loading of the second commences. Some slight movement on the cliff top on the other side of the creek catches Ellie's eye. Silhouetted against the brightening sky a horse and rider. In the moonlight the horse appears to be grey and the portly figure astride it, a man of the cloth. Could it be the Abbot from the priory? He is pointing to where the loading is taking place.

'What's got him involved?' Ellie ponders and then the realisation hits her. Friar Ignatius called the other day to collect tea, fish, rabbits and pheasants -----a fortnightly arrangement with the Abbot in exchange for a 'blind eye' and a few eggs and the odd chicken. When he enquired if Jo could get some brandy for the Abbot, Ellie peevishly answered, "You want brandy? You best ask that wench Maggie at the Inn. She has it all." It is suddenly obvious that Friar Ignatius has relayed her careless remark back to the Abbot. The Abbot being annoyed that he cannot get any brandy decides to inform on Jo to the Excise authorities. At least he'll have the reward money. Ellie realises Jo is in grave danger and this makes her panic. All thought of revenge is forgotten. Should she shout a warning to Jo and incriminate herself? Ellie is desperately trying to work out what is for the best ----- when her thoughts are shattered by the short, sharp crack of a musket shot and a howl of pain.

Sid, one of the gang, falls to the shingle beach clutching his stomach. The remaining horse whinnies and rears up within its shafts spilling some of the contents of the cart. The gang members drop to the beach taking what cover they can. Jo, without regard for his own safety, rushes to Sid's side and drags him out of sight behind the cart. A second bullet whistles

5

past his ear. From beneath the cart, Jo also spies the lone horseman. He would know that grey anywhere and its owner.

"Bastard," he swears under his breath. "I'll have you for this, Abbot."

There is no need for quiet any longer so Jo directs his gang to adopt their alternative plan. Using the horse and cart as cover and leaving the contraband, they hastily attempt the steep side of the creek. Sid is unceremoniously heaved onto the back of the cart. Jo keeps between them and from whence the shots came, in order to return fire if necessary. No attack comes so Jo retreats cautiously.

After much effort, they manage to push the cart to the top of the cliff. Hopping aboard they persuade the willing horse to gallop off as fast as it can muster. Sid still moans. Their progress is good on the firmer ground and they should reach the rendezvous fairly soon. Jo is to meet them later.

***

Jo is still backing away, keeping a careful eye. Suddenly two Excise officers appear on the other side of the creek. They must have been hidden in the dunes. They are about to cross the stream making directly for Jo. Jo whips out one of the pistols tucked in his belt and fires. One officer screams in pain. The horses rear up almost unseating their riders. The injured officer fights to stay on. "Christ! Gordon, we're not paid enough by the King to risk our lives." Slouched over the neck of his steed and hanging onto its mane he rides off in the direction from whence he had come. Gordon follows on his heels.

Jo waits a minute or two. All is quiet again. He quickly moves up the creek. Ellie sees another horseman picking his way carefully down a gully on the opposite side. Jo cannot see him but the horseman will soon see Jo. Ellie yells a warning.

"Jo! Look out."

Jo spins around to trace the call. The Excise officer sees him and there is the crack of another musket shot. The scarlet tunic and golden epaulettes single the assailant out as the Officer in Command of the Excise unit. He charges across the shallow stream brandishing his pistol, which has replaced the musket. Jo has fallen to his knees. He is badly hurt. There is a flash from the pistol followed almost immediately by a small explosion. Jo feels a burning pain as the bullet rips into his body. The steed is quickly closing on Jo. The officer now has a sabre in his outstretched arm ready for the final slash. There is a deep throated growl; primeval, sinister and a black streak hurls itself at the horseman. The sabre flashes in the moonlight. A yelp from the hound as steel cuts through flesh and bone. The horse shies unseating its rider. The officer is flung to the ground and tries to stagger to his feet but is dazed and shaken. Jo is not going to give up without a fight. His second pistol is in his hand. His aim is true. The Excise officer goes down. His last spluttering words, "I always thought it was you Fisherman Jo. Leader of the John Barrel Gang."

Ellie witnessing all that is unfolding rushes down to help her man. Half running, half stumbling, she reaches Jo breathless. The officer is dead. Shuck, motionless, head between his front paws as if asleep, laying in his own blood. Jo at the brink of death. Carnage, blood and gore, everywhere. Large patches of dark stained sand. Ellie looks down on her Jo. His face is deathly pale and etched with lines of pain. She drops down beside him and eases his head gently onto her lap.

"My Jo.-----My darling-----My love. What have I done to you?" she sobs. "Please forgive me."

Jo's eyes flutter open. He looks at her. Ellie sees the depth of pain but also the tenderness and knows then that she is the one he loves. With great effort he reaches up and touches her face with her fingers. She covers his hand with hers and presses it to her cheek. His eyes close. He is gone. Ellie kisses his forehead and wipes the trickle of blood from the side of his mouth. Then she kisses his lips remembering how warm they always were.

Ellie does not know how long she sits there with Jo's head in her lap. Everywhere is quiet and she is alone with her thoughts and memories. It must have been some time because the moon is high and she is suddenly aware that she is cold. Her mind is numb with sorrow but she knows she must get back to the cottage before being discovered. Ellie gives Jo one last kiss before rising slowly. She leaves Jo and Shuck and wends her way back towards the cottage. A fox barks. An owl hoots. Neither registers with Ellie but then another sound does. Is there something behind her? She listens intently. There it is again ----- soft but clear. Now Ellie is afraid but too far from home to run. 'Turn and confront it,' is her advice advice to herself, so turning quickly she is shocked to see Shuck a few paces behind.

"What are you doing here? I thought you were dead."

The dog wags its tail. Strangely, Ellie feels a lot safer now that Shuck is with her. They walk together, the hound always slightly behind until they reach their garden gate. Ellie holds it open for Shuck to come through after her. The hound holds back on the path and raising its head up to the moon it lets out the most piteous of howls, then bounds away, disappearing into the night.

Ellie never sees Shuck again. Often though, before retiring for the night, Ellie feels she hears a mournful, distant howl from up on the heath or down by the cove. The folk around know not to cause Ellie any harm and Ellie feels as secure as she ever did in her remote cottage.

Hello everyone, my name is Ben Larkins. I am 25 years old and live in Ipswich with my family and friends.

I work full-time and enjoy writing inbetween work and my raving social life. I have loved writing since a very young age; I was always writing stories as a kid. In fact, for the past ten years, my friend and I have been writing a series of stories, which we would one day love to get published.

I have written the story you are about to read and I hope you like it. I would like to thank Sandy and my fellow writers for their creative lessons we have taken part in and I hope you enjoy their great work too.

Remember my name, you will see it again! Happy reading and remember to stay creative!

The Journey

The whole world knows me, well think they know me. They have no idea though, no idea what crazy thoughts are swirling around in my head because I know that this is the last day of my life.

I think back to the comments I got when I graduated high school all those years ago. I remember it clearly; it was one of those days that you remember forever. All of us, wherever life may lead us, and whatever journey we would embark on, would remember it. I remember my classmates voted me winner for the award of 'Most Likely NOT to succeed in life', when we graduated forty-five years ago. I chuckle to myself at that thought now, 'Most likely NOT to succeed in life ', ha-ha!

I am currently sitting in my Californian mansion, while my maid cleans downstairs and only just over a month ago, I completed work on, roughly, my one hundredth studio picture. I am not one to boast. I don't believe in that. I think it's stuffy and not the way to be. I hate the lifestyle of the rich and famous. All these uptight bastards who think they are better than everyone else just because they have a few million in the bank. I don't feel the need to tell everyone I'm worth that, it's no one's business but mine and my bank manager's after all! 'Most likely NOT to succeed' though, eh? I think I've done pretty alright for myself if a million dollar lifestyle and worldwide fame is to go by. Oh but sometimes, just sometimes, that's just not enough.

I was born into a relatively middle class family, on July 21st 1951. Mother said I came into the world kicking and screaming, as loud and bubbly as ever and knowing what I wanted. She apparently knew I was destined for 'greatness'. Ah, bless Mother!

Mother was a model from Jackson, Mississippi, and my father was a senior car sales executive. He managed to rake in the money to support me, my mother and my two older brothers. We did move around a lot, but I guess with my father getting a new position at his job, that was to be expected. I attended a public school though so we weren't exactly a standard 'rich' family by any stretch. I was never really outgoing at school to be honest which is kind of hard to believe when you see what I end up doing with myself, believe me. My teacher, Mrs Burton, used to tell my parents that I was pretty shy and quiet but excelled at all my work! Ha, that's funny also when you see what journey I ended up taking myself on.

It wasn't until I got involved in the drama department at high school that I began to overcome my shyness. Something about being able to clown around and be someone else appealed to me. I didn't know why at this point but it just did, it was fun! After years of making mother laugh;

and I admit now it was to take some attention away from my older brothers, I began to try some jokes on my fellow classmates and friends. It was great for trying to impress the girls, or so I thought, until I realized girls seemed to like the jocks and the guys on the sports team. 'Well, I will join the goddamn sports team then!' I decided. It was a smashing success and I ended up playing for the school soccer team and the wrestling team. I can honestly say I loved it, though I have always been a bit of a perfectionist, so was determined to win whatever I was playing at. Wrestling was always good fun. My brothers and I used to play wrestle when we were younger whilst Mother and father were at work.

My dear mother used to say, "You are a funny boy!" which is probably why, after trying to make her laugh throughout my childhood, I decided I would give it a go at being a stand-up comedian.

Making people laugh can't be that difficult can it? I mean, what's the worst that could happen? You get booed off stage or ridiculed? I may as well give it a go, especially if it's something that I've loved doing ever since I can remember!

Jonathan Winters was my main inspiration to delve into the world of comedy. My god, I used to roar with laughter at him when I was as young as eight. He became my idol. I wanted the reaction that he got for my own work. I made it my mission to break the comedy circuit. I started trialling on mother. She always laughed, but then most mothers compliment their son's jokes don't they? Jonathan Winter's work inspired me so much. He made me believe that anything is possible and that anything in everyday life can be funny. He gave me the idea that comedy can be free-form and that you can go in and out of things pretty easily, covering all kinds of topics. I also admired the late Richard Pryor, mainly because he seemed fearless with his topics whilst on stage, covering his personal life such as his drink and drug abuse. But I didn't need to worry about that did I?

I was an aspiring comedian using all these skills to help me with my work. I practiced for years; all through high school I would try out new material on my classmates, hence why when we graduated in 1969, they voted me 'funniest' and 'least likely NOT to succeed', something that I still giggle about sometimes.

I ended up going to college at Julliard School after that, where I met my best friend and one of the kindest guys you could ever meet, Christopher. We were roommates and were on the same Drama course together, so we instantly hit it off! I remember the two of us were the only ones selected for the Advanced Programme in Drama. Ms Skinner our dialect coach was apparently in awe of me, as I managed to pick up all types of dialect and accent. I was just giving it a go and enjoying the ride. Christopher was brilliant to me, he really was. I remember he would even share his food with me when I had no money, bearing in mind he didn't have much money either - that was a kind thing to do. We remained friends right through college and supported each other's work.

I remember the first stand-up I did. I was terrified and felt sick inside but knew I could keep talking and keep the audience entertained. I had to! This was what I wanted to do! After begging all around San Francisco, I finally persuaded the manager of the comedy club 'Holy City Zoo' to give me a job. I worked the bar firstly but soon managed to talk my way into a stand-up show. I was terrified but had my material ready, and years of practicing to get me through. Thank god it went down well, I was on such a high afterwards and even more so when I got offered more gigs. I was doing it. I was reaching my dream.

The more gigs I did, the more material I knew I would have to have prepared. I was never one for writing a script though, or even following it. Christopher used to laugh at me in college for improvising and going off script in order to get a belly chuckle out of everyone. They were fun times.

The stress of preparing my shows was what started it, what got me hooked on a little thing called cocaine. Stand-up is a brutal field and

15

back in the 70s I was using regularly, too regularly if I'm honest. It was the lifestyle I thought I wanted: partying, drink and drugs. You know you are making it when you're living that kind of lifestyle, right? How wrong I was. Alongside my shows, I continued to work the bar, as that was my job, and I was meeting all sorts of people: drug addicts, alcoholics and general nasty bastards. I was with a bad crowd. Until I met her. Whilst bar working I met Valerie, she was beautiful, kind and not your typical hooker types that were regularly in the clubs. She was special, and soon enough we were an item.

In 1977, the two of us moved from San Francisco to Los Angeles. Christopher had been working hard there himself and we regularly met up whilst I was getting higher profile gigs. He had just been cast in a breakthrough role in a motion picture. I was so pleased for him.

It was one night after a performance in one of the LA clubs, that I had a knock on my dressing room door. A man I had never seen before introduced himself as George Schlatter. He was a TV producer and had loved my show so much that he asked me to appear in a new TV venture of his, a comedy show called 'Laugh In'. Valerie was telling me to go for it; this would be exposure to millions of people. She told me my 'talent to make people happy' had to be shared. So I agreed and did the show. I wasn't that nervous. I had spent years doing stand-ups. You kinda forget the cameras are rolling and millions of others are watching you. The show didn't do great, in fact, it failed with the mainstream audience, but it exposed me to the world of television and opened up doors for me I didn't realize existed beforehand.

In 1978, my agent was contacted by the producer Garry Marshall of the sitcom 'Happy Days'. They had seen my work and wanted me for a guest part in an episode. 'I have to make them remember me!' I kept telling myself as I walked into the audition and when they asked me to take a seat I thought I would do the opposite and sit on my head! They laughed. I spoke to them seriously whilst remaining on my head. Like I said, I hate to big myself up, but that audition changed my life. They gave me the guest part of an alien man in the show, a part which viewers apparently 'loved' and 'wanted more of', which led to me being asked by the network if I would like to be in a spin-off of the same character. 'Oh my god, are you serious?! I was ecstatic. I must have partied for weeks after accepting. My liver didn't know what had hit it. I was so overwhelmed I asked Valerie to be my wife, which she agreed to. We married the June of 1978. I then began work on the show, a show I am forever known for even to this day...

17

The show was an instant hit getting weekly figures of 60 million. I thought back to that innocent prediction at my graduation, 'most likely NOT to succeed.'

I continued to do stand-up, and stupidly the drink and drugs were constant too. I admit I should have realized I had a good thing going; my career was on the up I had a beautiful wife and was making great friends in LA.

The show ran from 1978-1982, when both I, my co-stars and the writers decided to end it. Mother always told me 'It's best to end things on a high rather than drag the damn thing out.'

I was being offered roles in Hollywood movies, my first role was in a low budget comedy in 1977 but my first leading role was in a film based on an old cartoon series. The film didn't do great but I was branching out, and I was enjoying the ride.

1983 is when everything changed for me with the birth of my son Zachary. I could not believe the love I had for this tiny baby. Reality hit hard and I realized if I continued my lifestyle I would miss out on my son's childhood. Valerie was growing tired with my mood swings. I couldn't see what I had done to our marriage. We had a young son and I was being offered parts in Hollywood films whilst still doing stand-up shows where I could. I even helped organize and teamed up with fellow comedians, and now dear friends Billy Crystal and Whoopi Goldberg, in 1986 for Comic Relief. As of present the cause raised $80 million. That feeling of helping somebody whether it be through charity work or something else is special. We are all the same after all and should help each other where we can; I'm a great believer in that.

I turned to exercise after I gave up drugs and drink, and slowly Valerie and I grew apart. We divorced in 1983. I now had a son to support, he was my world. I continued to work; now I was classed as a 'movie star' as they say. It wasn't long before I realised I was attracted to Zak's nanny, Marsha. God, she was beautiful, her dark hair and exotic features mesmerised me. It wasn't long before she was in my bed. We were married in 1989 and soon two more children followed. My daughter Zelda was born in 1989 and my son Cody in 1991. Life seemed to be going good; my film roles were increasing, including a reimagining of Peter Pan in a Steven Spielberg movie, a radio jock in a Vietnam War movie and a Scottish cross-dressing nanny!

It was 1995 when I was told that Christopher, my lifelong friend, had been in a horse riding accident and was severely paralysed. I visited him in the hospital. He could not move. His dear wife Dana told me Christopher had stated he wanted to die. I felt helpless, all the times he had looked

19

after me in college. I felt helpless, what could I do to make this pain bearable for my dear friend? So I did the only thing I knew how to, the very thing he supported me doing from the day we met, I made him laugh.

I dressed as a Russian Doctor and entered his room, muttering in a hyperactive manner and bouncing about, acting like a lunatic. It worked. Christopher couldn't stop laughing. I assured him I would help with all his medical bills and be there for him, just like he had always been for me. I could see the appreciation in his face, as he managed a smile. It was this that inspired me to audition for a high profile serious role in a movie, one that I got, much to the surprise of my critics. The role was of a psychiatrist helping a troubled youngster with his problems; something I was all too familiar with. To my shock I won the academy award for 'Best Supporting Actor' at the Oscars the following year. It was one of the highlights of my career. I thought back to my graduation, 'Most likely NOT to succeed' and a smile etched across my face. Up yours doubters!

Christopher fought on until 9 years later. On October 10th 2004 he passed away due to heart failure. He was 52. To say it hit me hard was an understatement. I had my work, my motion pictures and my stand-up. I had my beautiful family. To watch my children growing up gave me a sense of complete wonder, seeing them grow into extraordinary human beings and thinking... 'They are mine.' But one thing I no longer had was my best friend. The grief of losing him and remaining strong in front of my family and friends drove me back to alcohol. I remembered the promise I made to myself when Zak was born, no more drugs. I kept that promise! Drink, however, I was not as disciplined with.

It was affecting my marriage to Marsha – we were arguing constantly. The film roles began to dwindle, with not as many blockbusters that I had been used to in the decade or so previously. In 2006, realizing I needed help, I checked into rehab. The doctors told me I had depression and the idiot that I am I continued drinking. Rehab helped me gain some grasp on reality though and I was soon out and back to work. Marsha and I separated in 2008. I had two failed marriages and three children under my belt. My children were my soul and I adored all three of them.

I was getting older, my film roles were a few gems here and there and others I just did for the money. After Zak was born I started to exercise, cycle really; I continued with this but I was getting older and in 2009, I had to postpone one of my stand-up shows due to a heart problem, something I had never had to do before. That got to me greatly! I felt I had let down my fans, fans that had stuck through me over the course of my career. In 2011, I married for what would be the third and final time, my wife Susan. She was a graphic designer and wasn't into the Hollywood lifestyle. I needed that. My kids loved her and although they were now young adults themselves they got on amazingly. I felt so incredibly lucky. When all my children and my wife were together, those were the moments I was glad to live for.

Sure enough the critics attacked me for the low box office performance in my recent movies and I turned back to drink. I didn't mean to, I knew what it had done to me before but I just wanted the pain to go away, the pain I felt when the expectations others had of me failed; expectations that I didn't seem to be fulfilling.

I was a perfectionist since childhood; this was something Christopher often laughed at me for. My bank manager informed me that my balance was at the lowest it had been in decades. Only months ago I was admitted to hospital and diagnosed with the early stages of Parkinson's disease. For me, that was it. I would not be able to carry on doing the only thing I had ever loved...making others laugh.

I was having panic attacks and although Susan and my children have been nothing but loving and supportive, I now saw how Christopher felt after his accident. I would rather end things my way than let a disease cripple me and stop me doing what I loved.

It's currently 11th August 2014 as I prepare to end this tremendous life of mine. As I tighten my belt around my neck at my Californian mansion, I would ask you to remember a speech from a movie I did, 'Jack', about a young boy who ages four times quicker than normal. My character read this speech at his graduation. Quite appropriate really seeing as at my graduation I was voted 'Most likely NOT to succeed' in life.

"Please, don't worry so much because in the end none of us have very long on this Earth. Life is fleeting, and if you're ever distressed, cast your eyes to the summer sky, where the stars are strong across the velvety night. When a shooting star streaks through the blackness turning night, make a wish and think of me and make your life spectacular...I know I did."

That line is one I could not improvise, but one in which every word rings true to me. My life has been spectacular. I am touched by all the joy others say I have brought them around the world. Remember, whenever you feel sad, do glance to the sky and think of me. I was voted 'Most likely NOT to succeed' and I don't know about you, but I think I did pretty well.

I have been Robin Williams.

Thank you for an incredible journey and remember to always follow your dreams.

23

Linda K Wilson

I love to write poetry, prose, witty verses, etc. I live in Suffolk near woodlands; hence I call myself the 'woodland poet'. I have always written, but have never tried to get anything published. There will always be a novel in the back of my mind.

It's been an *unusual* few weeks; thanks Sandy.

Bitter Sweet

You're beautifully packaged, and I turn a blind eye to the warnings about how strong or how weak you are, and that you might kill me. I pay no heed because I am addicted to you. When people criticise you, I praise you and say what a calming effect you have on me in times of stress. I can't understand why people don't want you around.

We go to swish restaurants, and even though you're wearing your silver or gold jacket, you're still frowned upon. After a meal I am breathless for you, and take you in the palm of my hand - your silver jacket cool to the touch - out to the restaurant garden. My tongue reaches out for your golden tip as I slip you from your silver jacket, flick the switch, and watch you blush, glowing red at the tip. I draw you in deeply, exhaling, watching you swirl dreamily toward the night sky.

It was so much more civilised in the old days when restaurants and cafés would be expecting you; the tables set with grooved glass so that I could lay you down between courses. I remember the movies when it was glamorous being seen with you, and we were welcome in the cinema and theatres.

My friends don't like you; they say you smell, and taint everything. They get jealous when we leave them at a table and wander out into the garden.

It's you I reach for when I awake, and of course my dark companion, hot, aromatic and sweet in his white porcelain; you complement each other. I sip the sweetness, draw you in, exhale, watching you dance and billow in silver-blue swirls and circles.

I used to be able to take you to the office, and reach for you whenever a niggling situation cropped up. Now, we go to the office car park, even when it rains, and I shield you with my umbrella. It's unbearable when your white suit turns dull and limp in the rain and you begin to bend.

It's been a busy morning. We met briefly at 10. With my dark companion in one hand, and you in the other, I feel relaxed.

I don't know how I've made it through until lunchtime; my head is spinning. It's you first, then lunch. Sometimes you are all I need. You are so good for me. I am super slim in my secretarial suit.
Lunch is finished, and I can't wait to meet again at 3pm. I'll bring chocolate and his dark companion.

Three has come and gone and the afternoon drags on.

At last it's five, the end of a long working day, and we're together again. My head's been in over-spin for the last fifteen minutes. We've got to sneak out sooner!

Anyway, we have an evening ahead uninterrupted; Beaujolais, you and me. Yes, I've invited Beau; he's full bodied and robust in his red livery. I crave you even more when Beau's around. I'll sip his sweetness, and sink into the sofa. You'll be glowing all night, dancing and swirling around my head, filling the air with rings and spirals. I'll lay you down sometimes in the groove of cool blue grass, watching, as you snake upwards in a straight line, then pirouette to bronze the ceiling.

Around one in the morning I'll take you to bed. Beau's gone but he's left me wanting and needing you more than ever. I lay back, draw you in, exhaling Beau vapour and watch your skittish dance through bloodshot eyes.

Then my friends introduced me to Patch (though not a patch on you!) They love to see him on my arm. He's with me day and night. Beau's gone too. Evian's here now. He's so cool and refreshing.

I'd hardly know that you were ever around. The ceiling is now white. My mind is clear. I've put on weight. My friends are here.

There are fleeting moments when I think of you, and feel a tinge of sadness, a bitter sweet memory.

26

Stolen

There is no choice
Mother standing at the door
Says 'goodbye'
In a small voice
Thinking,
'I won't see him anymore.'
He's only nineteen
He's young, he's keen
He thinks it's thrilling
To do some killing
But there is fear, there is dread
Seeing his friends shot down dead
Watching children playing ball
Hearing their cries when they fall
As bullets rip through their play
Blasting their young lives away
Feeling their pain as their limbs are torn
Seeing and hearing the mothers mourn
Seeing a father shot through the head
As he watches his newborn being fed
The mother's cries are shrill and raw
Not heard a sound like this before
Gutters run red with the wounded and dead
No doctors, no hospital bed
There's no call for white poppies, please
White poppies will not bring us peace
They must remain forever red
That's how we will remember our dead

La Pucelle

She replied, 'The Voice was gentle, soft and low and the figure was bathed in light.'

Her judges were angry, saying, 'This could not be so!' Her lips did not move. To her it's spiritual...to them what could she prove?

'Was the Voice straight from God, an angel or saint - male or female?' Her reply, 'It's the Voice of St Catherine, St Margaret, St Michael.'

Aged twelve, it was midday summer in her father's garden when she heard the Voice of God.

'To help me, and guide me', she said, but the judges railed, 'It's all in her head!'

In January 1412, this girl was born in Domremy on the River Meuse on the borders of Lorraine to peasants Jacques and Isabelle. It was a life of persistence, determination, bravery and pain.

They would always ask for a sign.

But why should she? Her instruction came from the Divine.

'Glasdale! Glasdale! Surrender to the King of Heaven! You call me a whore but I have great pity for your soul. The King of Heaven orders and notifies *you* through *me*. You, men of England, flee!'

They called her fanciful, heretic, witch, liar, yet she always spoke with clarity and calm, remaining firm and did not tire, with no thought that she would come to harm. She was confident and knew that it was right when the Voice she heard commissioned her to fight.

When injured, soldiers offered to treat her wound with a charm.

'I would rather die, than do a thing I know to be against the will of God!' she replied, still confident, determined and calm.

Victory at Orleans saw Charles VII crowned. At the coronation, she was given a place of honour next to the king.

She had a banner on which was sown with lilies in a field - *she knew that she would never yield --- -* there represented was the World, the image of God holding the World with two angels at the sides, and written upon it 'Jesus, Mary'.

28

When asked who told her to have her banner - painted as it had been,

'By God's command', she answered in courteous manner. I did nothing but by God's command. I went forward to take the land and I bore this standard against the enemy to avoid killing anyone.'

But this they could not see.

She is the only person, whether girl or man, to hold command of a nation's military forces, aged only seventeen, since written human history began. She still brings us to tears, and it is nearly seven hundred years.

Questioned again and again, her reputation put to shame.

Her famous response to a trick question:

'Are you in God's grace?'

'If I am not, may God put me there,

And if I am, may God keep me there,

I should be the saddest creature in the world

If I knew I were not.'

This young girl does not lose face.

God takes the foolishness and weakness of a man and turns it into genius and strength as no one else can.

She became a soldier without sword, armour, or even a horse. She could neither read nor write, yet twenty letters were written - with God to pre-empt in this cause - dictated with clarity and might.

In fourteen hundred and thirty she was captured whilst defending Compiegne. By the Burgundians she was bought and they hurled their loathing for her male attire when handed over to an ecclesiastical court. How dare she? It was an offence to the church. That *they* offended God, they paid no heed.

A closed mind, not clothes is to besmirch. A church is nothing - for God they had no need.

And now convicted in fourteen hundred and thirty-one, and burned at the stake in Rouen marketplace. There was no safe place to where she could run. Where was the man who now was king? No attempt to come to *her* rescue, and spare her death's sting.

On that fateful day she still showed concern for Rouen as they lead her away.

'Must I die here? Ah, Rouen I fear, you will have to suffer for my death.'

'Hold the crucifix before my eyes, so I may see it until I die.'

I imagine the agonising cries.
The last words she uttered were
'Jesus, Jesus, Jesus!'

In fourteen hundred and fifty-six, there was a second trial, with no biased judges with their ignorant evidence. This time there would be no denial and at last a pronouncement of her innocence.

She was always clear that her instruction was from the Divine, and justice prevailed when she was beatified in nineteen hundred and nine. In nineteen hundred and twenty without prejudice or complaint, she was officially declared to be a Saint.

My pen name is Amaranthia. I live in a tiny village in rural Suffolk with my husband, three grown up children, Springer spaniel and rabbit. As well as writing I also enjoy needlework and jewellery making. 'The Inheritance' was originally penned for my 'O' Level English Language mock exam more years ago than I care to remember! It has been updated and extended especially for this Anthology.

The Inheritance

I turned as the taxi cab drove off up the narrow country lane. In front of me stood an impressive pair of fancy wrought iron gates, strung across from stone pillars that were topped with a stone horse head. An engraved stone plaque announced the name of the property, along with a carving of acorns and oak leaves. Impressive!

My thoughts turned back to the previous week when I received a letter from a firm of solicitors that I had never even heard of. The pristine white envelope, with its gold crest on the reverse, dropped on the floor along with the usual quantity of junk mail that I seemed to amass daily. I had picked it up, staring at the crest, wondering why such a prestigious envelope should find its way through my door. Surely, it was a mistake, meant for someone else - not for me! There was only one way to find out. I opened it carefully and could scarcely believe the content of the enclosed letter.

It would seem that an uncle that I had not seen since I was a little girl had died and left me his house and stables, deep in the countryside. There was also a grand sum of money that would enable me to take up this property and not have to sell it because I would be unable to afford its upkeep. True, he had no children of his own to leave it to, but never in a million years would I expect to receive this sort of windfall.

I had ridden as a child, though I was never lucky enough to have my own horse. I spent many hours at the local stables helping look after my four legged friends in return for a weekly riding lesson.

33

Grooming, mucking out, and cleaning tack were relished in all weathers. What young girl didn't dream of having her own horse one day in the distant future? Perhaps he had left it to me, as I was the only one in the family who would have a clue as to what to do with it, other than sell it. I would certainly appreciate the chance to change my life.

There were instructions to visit the solicitor's office to sign some papers and collect the keys to the property. There was also a return ticket for the train from my local station. It was for First Class travel. Now that would be a novelty! I felt as if I were in a dream. Surely, I would wake up any time now and find this was all a product of my vivid imagination.

Today had finally arrived. When you are excited and looking forward to something, why does time seem to pass so slowly? I left my battered old Mini in the station car park and caught the train as instructed. The journey was straightforward. It was quiet and comfortable in the forward compartment. Plenty of legroom as I watched first the town and then the countryside whizz by through the carriage window. I could get used to this!

The train arrived on time. I had disembarked and gone to wait under the station clock. There on a seat sat a young man in a suit. As I approached the seat, he stood up and greeted me by name. Having established that I was who I should be, he led me out of the station to a waiting car, ready to whisk me off to the solicitor's office.

Their office was in an old Tudor listed building situated in a quiet alleyway. Stepping through the entrance to the building was almost like travelling back in time. The sofas in the reception area were large and old fashioned, made from quality leather. A large fresh floral arrangement sat in the fireplace. The receptionist sat at an

34

old-fashioned desk that was a statement piece of furniture. The telephone and laptop looked decidedly out of place in their surroundings. They gave the impression of something from the modern world that had intruded into the quiet calm atmosphere. Having just got comfortable with a magazine from the low coffee table, I was cordially invited to follow her through to the 'inner sanctum'.

The solicitor waiting to see me was quite elderly with snow-white hair and a twinkle in his eye. Having requested coffee and biscuits from the receptionist, he sat me down and talked me through the legacy bequeathed to me. My earlier theory was correct. His estate had all been left to me, as my uncle believed that I was the only person in the family that he felt could truly appreciate the gift.

I was told that my uncle had been a recluse for many years but had spoken of remembering me as a child, although he had not had visitors for many years. Purchases were delivered and the resulting bills sent to the solicitor's for payment. This elderly professional, who must surely be beyond retirement age himself, had been his only contact with the outside world. He explained to me that there were no longer horses there now, but that everything at the property would now belong to me.

There were numerous forms for me to sign and although he had keys for me now, the accounts would need time to be transferred to my name. As part of the legacy I had the use of his services for the following few months. Hopefully through him I would learn a little more of someone I could barely remember. When we'd finished, I walked out of there feeling both dazed and excited. I headed straight for a taxi – I was keen to see just what was waiting for me.

35

My thoughts came back to the present with a jolt. My hand slipped into my coat pocket. There I found the small remote control that had been given to me along with the keys. I pointed it towards the gates and pressed the button. At first, nothing seemed to be happening and then slowly, with a low hum, the gates opened. Oak Farm beckoned.

The place was aptly named. On both sides of the long drive were green paddocks containing several mature oak trees. They were so big and grand that they were probably young saplings when William the Conqueror had invaded Britain. Solid post and rail fencing separated them from the drive. I could see the house at the end of the long drive where it opened up into a large gravelled area. The house was timbered and very picturesque. An open front porch gave protection to a solid oak studded door. Small windows contained leaded panes. Suddenly it all felt real – this was now my house! This was the place that I would learn to call home. The solicitor had offered for someone to come and show me around, but I knew that I wanted to do this by myself. This was to be a special moment and I wanted to discover everything for myself. I was like a small child let loose in a candy store.

As I walked up to the front door, keys in hand, I changed my mind. The house could wait for later. I wanted to see the stables first. I turned and strode over to an archway. It led to a walled garden. Spaced out along one wall were square openings each with a hinged door. I could imagine proud equine heads looking out of the glassless window that was sheltered from cold winds. A further arched doorway took me through to the stable yard. As well as the stables, there were storage rooms for tack and feed. A large barn stood a little way off.

36

I opened one of the stable doors and looked inside. Inside they were clean, light and airy. There was no trace of the previous occupant. A heavy iron hayrack sat in one corner and in another a rounded rectangular manger for feed. There was also an automatic drinker for water. Obviously, no expense had been spared, the loose box was well appointed, designed around the horses that should live there.

I continued exploring, and my feet took me to the large barn. In addition to the barn doors, there was a small door to one side. I opened it and peered in. The inside of the barn was divided into sections. One contained a tractor, complete with trailer, a small horse lorry, and various other mechanical aids. Another had been used to store hay - there was still a thin layer spread over the floor. The largest part had a deep layer of sawdust and had been used as an indoor exercise area for the horses that lived there.

Wherever I looked, everything was so perfect. There were so many possibilities, but I instinctively knew what I wanted to do with the place. I wanted to start up a breeding programme. The noble Arabian had always been my favourite. With dainty heads and long flowing manes, I always thought that they were beautiful. I was about to inherit more than enough money, not only to look after the place but also to realise a lifelong dream. With a contented sigh, I returned to the house. Perhaps after all this I ought to have a look at the house that was about to become the centre of my life!

My name is Vanessa Scott.

I never thought I'd see my work in print.

Enjoy!

A Forced Situation

I cannot explain this deep ocean of sadness inside me. It has presented itself in many ways, sometimes it shows up as a storm, tempestuous and furious, sometimes as a tsunami which drenches my whole body in grief; more frequently now, it is a calm pool on which my emotions sail.

I can't speak about what happened very easily but as I sit with my seat-belt buckled ready for the flight, my hand being clasped by Joe's, I know this physical journey, although the longest of my life, is nothing compared to the emotional journey which has exhausted my last three years.

Joe smiles at me as the pilot announces that we are due for take-off. One of those clipped, well spoken, English accents fills the cabin and I smile. I am excited that I am beginning a new life. There is not any part of me that wants to stay in Australia. Joe has changed my life.

My first memory of Joe was when he came into the café. Those soft brown eyes and that smile. Coffee and cake had been the brief order. I didn't realise it then, but he'd come in because he'd seen me. My crazy green pinafore, and my short chopped hair, was clearly an attraction.

He was friendly but it wasn't until he saw me the following week, crying on a bench, that we actually became friends. Most men would have run a mile. As I sat there, tears streaming down my face, without any answer to his queries of concern, he must have thought I was deranged. I was definitely messed up.

It wasn't long before he heard my story, and the strangest thing was he seemed angry for me. We moved in together a month later, to the flat he was renting short term. He was travelling the country. I felt there was nowhere I specifically belonged, so I went along for the ride.

At the time I met Joe, I was sharing a bedsit with Samantha. We had been through so much together. Our friendship had stopped us from becoming alcoholics or drug users; a fate left to other young girls in our situation.

Samantha and I had been together at the Centre, forced to work, coerced by the supervisors. We had both been disowned by our families and all for the crime of falling in love. We understood each other, felt a sense of belonging with each other, but mostly, we trusted each other.

The rest of my story would not make sense if I didn't introduce Paul. He was so good looking; I could have stared at him all day. Our moments were stolen after school, a shared cola from the shop, or splitting a Cherry Ripe in the sun. We would sit under the tree in the park, and talk about school, and kiss. We'd read together. I was sixteen; he was seventeen. We had been going out for 9 months, but my dad was strict and would not have entertained me having a boyfriend.

My dad, who I loved with all my heart, would I'm sure have liked Paul. Although I guess, knowing my dad, he would have put getting my higher school certificate before getting a boyfriend. My dad was proud of me, and wanted me to stay at school to do my HSC. I got good reports, I loved school, and, but for my obsession with Paul, English Literature would have been the only love in my life that competed with my dad.

The day they took me away, the day I saw the disappointment in my dad's eyes, was the day I knew I'd never see Paul again.

I remember those last few weeks before Jack was born. I would cradle my arms around my bump, hugging him to

40

ensure he knew my love, hugging him to safety. I remember I didn't want it to end. I wanted to keep him safe inside me, to stay connected. I talked to him every night, in soft whispers so the other girls in the dorm would not hear. I didn't want to lose him. I hadn't got over losing my dad from my life. I wished he still wanted to protect me.

His shame, or the shame I'd brought on him, and on my family, eclipsed his love for me. In three weeks, I would lose the only thing close to me and I cried each night at the pain of that burden. I felt the deep sorrow of knowing I would not be able to keep my baby. That's when I made friends with Samantha. She heard me whispering one night and told me she did that too. Hugging her bump was the closest she'd get to loving her baby, so she held on tight, hoping and praying he would want to stay warm and incubated.

He did not stay warm and incubated, neither did Jack. Our arms would only hug our bumps for a few weeks more. The day the pain came, I tried to pretend it hadn't. I tried to hide my contorted face from the supervisor with each contraction. I felt a sense of dread when she came to me and said 'Come child, it's your time'.

***

As I look at Joe now, flying toward my new life, tears well again. He is reading but with his hand resting on my thigh, as if to hold down the turmoil, which is once again, ready to resurface. He looks at me and says, 'Good riddance Australia', he squeezes my hand as we continue, 'we are going to build a new life for you, one with smiles and happiness and laughter'.

***

The only comforting thing I remember as I gave birth to Jack was the nurse who put a cool towel on my forehead. I

41

remember in flashbacks the efficiency of it all. No room for softness. Sobbing through my pain, wishing that my mum and dad were with me, wishing there was some love in the room. I knew they were right, that Jack was entitled to a good life, someone with the money and the support to give him opportunities. They said my mistakes did not need to ruin Jack's life. They said, even though I had done wrong, I could still make the right decision and give Jack a future.

As he entered the world, Jack wailed. I think he wanted me. I think he knew they were taking him away. I pleaded with them to let me hold him just once, to hug him. They wouldn't. A nurse explained it was for the best. An attachment would not help me let go. I did not want to 'let go'. He was my baby. As they stitched me, and took him away, I pleaded with them to let me see him. I just wanted to look at his face. They scurried him out of the room and thrust papers at me to sign.

As the pen scribbled, I realised that I would never be the one who kept him safe, never be the one to soothe his tears, or witness his first step and first word. I didn't know what the point of anything was any more.

The best thing from my time at the Centre was meeting Samantha, as I said; we kept each other safe, and kept each other living when we both felt there was no reason to go on. Once we had both healed, we had been sent on our way, released with twenty dollars.

***

Joe helped me see Australia before I left her shores. We had visited so many places together, earning money from temporary jobs.

We were going to England. It was December 1975. Despite everything that had happened to me, I was so grateful for Joe. He had given me a reason to consider a future. He'd told me about his sister, his mum and dad, and how annoying they were. They sounded great to me, so full of love and care. 'Well intentioned meddlers' said Joe. His family would become my family and maybe there would be children of our own. Mostly I was looking forward to Christmas in England. Would it snow? Would there be Christmas lights in the streets? Would it be freezing cold enough to see my own breath? Everything felt new and exciting.

The plane touched down and slowed to a stop. That clipped English accent was back "Well good evening everyone and welcome to London Heathrow, the air temperature outside is a balmy 7 degrees!" I giggled with all the anticipation of shedding the old and bringing in the new.

***

Thirty-one years later, as I hug Allie with all my heart, she says 'go for it mum'. She smiles at me with her dad's eyes. I love her. She has been so supportive and I promise I will call her when I arrive.

After several scanning machines (oh the curse of 9/11) I eventually make it through to the departure lounge. I am flying with Qantas, but duty free comes first.

The last thirty years have been amazing. I have been lucky. I was right about Joe, after thirty years of being my soul mate, twenty-eight of being my husband, and twenty-five of being a fantastic dad to Allie, Joe passed away last year. He was sick at the end; it was a very hard time for us.

Allie has kept me busy over the last few months, petitioning the Australian Government over what it did. Asking for records, asking for anything that would help me find my son, her half-brother.

We became women on a mission. A mission to right a wrong; a mission, I guess, to right several wrongs and the chance to explain to my son what had happened.

The world has changed since then, but there has still been no outright apology for what they did or for the lives they destroyed, and the pain they caused.

I now know that what they did was a far graver sin than what I did. My life in England, and the love it has brought me, has shown me that.

After what has felt like months of searching and questioning, and coming up against several brick walls, they have found my son and this is the reason I am going back.

As I board the plane, I hope to put behind me some of the grief that losing Joe has caused me. I know that he would be one hundred percent behind me if he were here.

I have spoken to Dan (he'll probably always be Jack to me), and it turns out I am a grandma.

I am even thinking of going to my old home. To see what happened to my parents. The years must have softened their hearts. I am my own person now, I do not need their love or their forgiveness, but I would like to see them again. To see if, with the passing of the years, and the way the world has changed, they regret their actions and the years we have lost.

I love my Allie, and my life in England, but it is with a renewed optimism I go home to Australia to pick up the pieces of a life I thought I had left behind. It's a second chance and I am full of hope.

Endnote:
News article from the Sydney Morning Herald on the 20 September 2012
O'Farrell says sorry for forced adoptions
NSW Premier Barry O'Farrell has said sorry for the "years of pain and grief" caused to mothers and to their children who were removed in past forced adoptions.

Delivering an historic apology at a joint sitting of parliament today, the premier said the practice had "reverberated through the lives of tens of thousands of mothers and their children who were removed".

More than a hundred people witnessed the apology from public galleries in the upper and lower house, and from the Strangers Dining Room.

Following an emotional reading from a mother, Lyn, whose son was forcibly adopted, Mr O'Farrell said the parliament acknowledged "the terrible wrongs that were done, and with profound sadness and remorse say to those living with ongoing grief and pain, we are sorry".

"The trauma induced by the forced adoption practices in the past has reverberated through the lives of tens of thousands of mothers, and their children who were removed," he told parliament.

"It's affected fathers who were never given a say, as well as the families who never knew of the truth of what went on with brothers, sisters, nieces and nephews or grandchildren they lost.

"It caused years of pain and grief for many instead of the joy and delight which parenthood might reasonably have been expected to bring."

The NSW apology follows similar apologies from the South Australian and Western Australian parliaments.

An estimated 150,000 Australian babies born between the 1950s and 1970s were taken from their mostly young and single mothers.

NSW Opposition Leader John Robertson said "there can be no excuse, there can be no justification" for the state-sanctioned forced adoptions of the past.

"Today we must step forward and take responsibility," Mr Robertson said.

"This single, barbaric act - fraying the sacred bond between mother and child - changed lives, and in many cases it destroyed them.

"On behalf of the NSW Labor opposition I rise to join with the government to say clearly and unequivocally to all those affected by the policy of forced adoption, we are sorry."

"We apologise to the mothers who were not asked or listened to.

"We apologise for making you feel ashamed and unfit to care for your babies.

"We say sorry for treating you cruelly and insensitively when what you needed and deserved most was care and support."

Mr O'Farrell apologised to those who had been forcibly adopted as children "who grew up never knowing the truth of your birth or how much you were wanted or loved by your mothers".

The apology was long overdue, he said.

"I hope your journey of recovery of healing is made easier by what you've heard."

NSW Family and Community Services Minister Pru Goward said a NSW parliamentary inquiry in 2000 had called the practice of forced adoptions unethical and unlawful.

Thursday's apology acknowledged the trauma and pain caused by the thousands of forced adoptions, she said.

"It is true that there were thousands of young women in NSW who were persuaded or manipulated to accept that adoption was in the best interest of their child, but there are an unknown number for whom the persuasion became coercion - they are part of this apology," Ms. Goward said.

46

She said there were women who have told of signing adoption papers under heavy sedation when they didn't understand what they were doing.

"Others have claimed they were browbeaten over days, or their signatures forged or not even collected. Some have said they were told their babies had died, only to find out years later it was all a lie.

"They are part of this apology," Ms. Goward said.

One woman, Lyn, read a three-minute poem describing the pain and despair she has had to suffer after being forced to give up her son.

Fighting back tears and anger, Lyn told MPs and those in the public gallery that the grief of losing her son had not eased over the years.

"I lost the child for whom I grieve ... you forced us to live apart," she said.

"One thing I need you to know, pain ever-lasting does not show.

"To the outside world there is no sign, but the child you stole was mine."

My name is Angie. I live in a small Suffolk village with my two young sons. Fiction writing isn't my strong point; I prefer factual writing, as you will guess from my story, which is loosely based on fact. I enjoyed testing myself on fiction mixed with fact though and I may indeed, one day in the future, go down this road.

Virus

*I'm hot and curious and walk with intent along a red dust road to meet my
subject. The African sun beats down on my back through my short-sleeved blouse
relentlessly. The dry ochre residue on the primitive roads out here covers my
flatties but soon I will be at my destination. I am going to interview a woman,
Funanya Woloma, about the epidemic that affected her community and most of
the surrounding villages. A Sand grouse scuttles away from me and a lone African
cuckoo lets me know he is there.*

*At the end of the road, I come to a clearing as predicted by my contact in
Kailahun. Children giggle then disappear in the maize field behind three
rudimentary mud huts. In the foreground, a woman stirs something with a long
wooden stick in a large iron cauldron as beads of sweat glisten on her forehead.
In the shade of a large old Cotton tree, two adults stand softly talking. A bee
buzzes, agitated by the heat. The woman continues to stir. Seeing me, she looks
up. Her perfect white teeth produce a friendly smile.*

'Hello. Katie? I'm Funanya,' *she says confidently as I approach her. I am
taken aback.* 'Yes, hi there....Katie Nicholson.'

'Please, I will bring you some water. It is too hot today. You can sit here.'
She grabs hold of a three-legged stool.

'Oh...thank you. It's so nice to meet you at last, Funanya.'

*The slim dark skinned woman's hair is in the symmetrical 'snakes and ladders'
style, so popular with African women and the water she hands me is lukewarm but
I sip gratefully. Adults and children are barefoot as their feet are accustomed to
the baking earth, the stones and little thorns. Funanya tells me that one of the
adults under the tree is her mother. The old woman's eyes narrow and she
mutters something to her cohort.*

'A man from Daru he come, he come and tell me. He tell me a woman, a
important woman is coming, she is coming all the way from England to speak with
ME!'

I'm not important...what is important however, is what has happened here.

'Can you tell me what's been going on, Funanya? How did the disease affect
your community?'

'Of course... yes... thousands died'. As she talks she continues washing bowls
and cleaning other cooking items in readiness. 'People come in to the country
and try and help us. Even I had it, the disease, but the health workers, they pick
me up and they take me to the hospital. I am lucky. I am healthy now. My good

49

lord! How is life these days? Nobody ever get over the shock of losing a person to this virus. One day it came to visit West Africa; another day maybe one out of five in a family survived. And soon we knew this was a visitor that would stay. We have been getting on with our lives for a long time now but everything has changed for the people here. Forever it has changed them.'

Slowly Funanya continues, 'No, time will not heal these wounds.' She ladles the stodgy white porridge from the cauldron into six basic hand carved wooden bowls. 'Can I give you some Katie?' I feel it is rude to decline and take Funanya up on her offer. I notice she leaves herself out.

I cool the steaming gruel. 'So tell me, what does your day normally entail? What is your job, your standing in life?'

'I am a mother. I have children and even grandchildren who God blessed me with, so my days are full although my children, they are grown up now. In the mornings I take my bucket...' Funanya wipes her brow with the back of her hand. 'I go to the lake for fresh water. I fill my bucket and put it on my head. Even for me, it is so very hot, the sun here in Leone but I have to go,' *her words are matter-of-fact, eyebrows raised, whilst she scrapes out the huge witch's pot.* 'So I walk for two hours, then I come back and prepare and cook the food. Everyone is glad when I am back, they now can drink.'

The old woman from the Cotton tree has been listening, scaly legs stretched out with great difficulty on the sand. Her clawed hand fights off flies who want her leftovers. The other woman from the tree slurps up the last bit of porridge from her bowl hungrily.

'My girl, listen to me, you work too hard,' clawed hand interrupts her daughter, 'what would your father say about working too much?'

Funanya does not reply and continues from where she left off.

'So, this is what I do every day, seven days a week. My son, Obi, comes to add to the compost heap and he will look after my vegetables. But he works far far away. When he has worked for most of the week, he can only give me two hours, and then he takes his children back home with him. Then, every time they go, I miss them,' she laughs, then sips water briefly.

The old woman stares indignantly at her daughter.

'Does your son live nearby?'

Again the slim woman laughs covering her mouth. 'He has to walk two hours like me!'

The children are back singing and giggling.

50

'Children! Please... eat! It is almost cold!' *Funanya reprimands them. The three pretty girls, all with the snakes and ladders hair, obediently take the bowls and scurry to the welcome shade of the old tree.*

'My father', Funanya *finally looks towards her mother* 'he work hard, all day he work, I watch him with the sweat on his face. I watch him tired from working hard. I work like him, I make him smile.

'Pah! I tell you what your father would say!' Gagool carries on regardless, as though her daughter's words themselves were flies you could brush off. He would say, "Nanya! Even on the lord's day off you work!"

'I am like Job mama. Remember, from the Bible? He worked with little rest. I am also like my father. And like Job, I try to please *my* God, going about *my* daily work. And I'm sure my father would say I am just like him!'

'Job? God? What you are talking about? Stupid talk! You should take a break! You make yourself ill. Then the work will pile up, up to the top. What then? No one will do things for you! You are selfish!'

Then why can't YOU help me once in a while, Funanya's exhausted eyes seem to say.

'If your husband was here, you would be a different woman'; *the cynic is on a mission.* Your face it is tired. You look old, old like the tall tree. You will die! You work yourself to the grave. Then your children have no parents! Who will help me?' *She huffs.* 'Ever since that husband of yours,...he..that man...'

'I don't mean to be rude', *I interrupt, seeing no end to this seemingly age old debate,* 'but I only have a couple of hours - and I must be back in the city on time. Can you tell me about your husband Funanya? I mean, the disease, was it...?' *But Funanya is busy defending her husband.*

What do you mean that husband of mine, mama? He died from the virus! Are you saying all those people are to blame for dying? How could they help it?'

'Many run away from Daru! Across the border! A border does not stop the spreading! Of course there is blame!'

'But Kwaku, my husband, did not run away! What are you trying to say to me? Be careful what you say! Please. You are old now mama but you are not wise in this matter. Kwaku died because we cared here for his father who had the disease! You *blame* Kwaku for dying because he took his ill father under his wing? It was mostly I who looked after his father! My husband, God take his soul, don't speak bad of him, he was a good man, he have faith.'

51

'No, no, no...Don't speak to me about faith!' The elderly woman screeches. 'My faith it die a long time ago along when my husband die! I bury him, straight away I renounce God!'

'You know, my father cared, just like his son-in-law did,' Funanya's is the one whose angry words now know no bounds. 'Yes, both of them die a long time ago, God take their souls.' 'Papa was killed protecting you and my Kwaku, he was killed by an epidemic. Both men were heroes.'

'The people who did care', Funanya explains turning back to me fully, 'they come quickly and help many of us; to them we are grateful; they pick us up, me and Kwaku; take us to the hospital; I mean, they helped me survive, help me live. Poor kind Kwaku, what chance did he have?'

I am merely a spectator, not a BBC journalist on assignment. My research showed that deaths were in their thousands, twenty two thousand or more. Sierra Leone, or West Africa for that matter, was crammed with dead news statistics at the time, not dead people. For now, I must hear Funanya out. The international community, the governments in Europe and America were not interested. They came in to it all too late. In the beginning, some of the health workers contracted the virus and died, which put a strain on and disrupted the entire health care system. Then, the field hospitals and treatment centres were built about ten months too late; FAR TOO LATE; the corpses in the endless numbered graves outnumbered those who had died non-related deaths.

Then a couple of white people died and suddenly the world was all ears.

It disgusted me; to find out these truths made me sick to the core.

'But your God sent the disease!' *Gagool raged on, standing there, toothless and pointing... at me as well*, 'Your God, he kill thousands; he kill them. He kill our people...he...,'

Whilst some people did not believe the virus existed, others believed it was witchcraft, a trick fabricated by local governments to get blood from people; and others again got infected from washing the dead, which is their tradition but one of the main ways to spread it.

'No mama, actually I do not share your view. He *saved* me so I could look after my four sons, my three grandchildren.' *Funanya gazed lovingly at the children who had dumped their bowls in a plastic tub and ran off again.* 'So, my God is a good God who loves each and every one of us - even you.'

'But our young husbands were taken from us', the old heretic continues. There is no stopping her. 'If God was good, he would not have taken them. He sent the virus. Your precious God, you wait 'Nanya, he will let you down. You think because of all your hard work God is saving you a seat up there,' her arthritic finger dismissively stabbed the air, 'ha! When the ravens and the crows come', and her arm went up again like a preacher beseeching his congregation, you think you will be spared, spared from...what do you call it...purg-a-tery?'

Now Funanya's look told me she thought her mother had gone too far.
She looked fed up with the whole accusation, once and for all.

'Listen, my family is alive. My family is well! Lucky I meet Kwaku or I would have nothing. I see him in little Tema. Every day I see my husband in my granddaughter's eyes. I feel him near us. I never lost my faith in all the years! Now my faith it is even stronger! Yes!'

'Don't say to me listen!' *Funanya's acid-tongued mother continued, spitting venom.* 'Just hear my words. Ha! You will see...your God is a snake! You can keep it, your faith! Ha! One day you will die! I'm not listening to you! Me I'm going!' *And with a thrust of the shoulder, Gagool is off.*

'You don't need to believe in God to have faith!' *Funanya calls after her and turns to me,* 'you just need to believe, to be strong, believe in yourself...and maybe help out once or twice!' *She busies herself with tidying up. I stay silent and as I watch the woman go, bare calloused feet unsteady on red sand, her back crooked, her arm frail and bent, I wonder how I would feel in her situation. I don't wonder for long. She clears her throat, spluttering. Her arthritic thumb buries itself in next to her spine to help alleviate the pain; years of pain, backstabbing, blasphemous and bitter.*

***

The snake, feeling threatened, lunges at her, five hundred metres from her daughter's house. The thin skin punctures instantly. Two deep venomous holes, bruised and black blooded where fangs strike her poisonous, hate-filled body, ooze the onset of convulsive death, and in minutes, Gagool is gone.

53

Linda Allen – closer to a pension than a youth club, but still undecided about what to do when she grows up. This is Linda's first attempt at writing a story for others to read since school days. She would like to thank Sandy Wolton and the Creative Writing Group for the support and encouragement they've given her in having a go at this writing game and hopes the reader enjoys her contribution.

The Piper Plays the Tune

Eleanor Franklin could barely hold back the tears as she knelt to hug her son and daughter. They stood on the platform with hundreds of parents and children doing a similar thing. The steam engine huffed and chuffed as it waited for the mass of juveniles to board its carriages. There was a slight chill as dawn had not yet broken, and Eleanor was glad the children had their winter coats on. At their feet were two small suitcases containing nightwear, underwear, toothbrush, comb, soap and face flannel. Gas masks hung across their shoulders.

"Now, you both behave yourselves, and have a good holiday in the countryside. And remember to send me that postcard when you get there."

"But, mum why can't you come with us?" Ten-year-old Jessica sobbed miserably as she clung to her mother's neck, whilst five-year-old Billy stood in bewilderment, fiddling with the luggage label pinned to his coat lapel. Why were so many people crying, he thought. We're going on holiday aren't we?

"Well, it's a special treat for you kids, like I said. You'll have a great time. Now don't make a fuss Jessie, you'll be alright." Eleanor stroked her daughter's hair and kissed her forehead.

"Anyway, you'll be back in a couple of weeks. Now promise me you'll look out for Billy, yes?" Jessica sniffed loudly and nodded. Her mother reached into her pocket for a handkerchief.

"Come on love. Here, use this and get onto that train with your brother."

Eleanor kissed her children one more time before they mounted the steps to join the others. Those who could leaned out of the open windows, others pressed their faces to the glass, waving and shouting farewell as the train pulled away from the station, whistle blowing in salute. Those left standing on the platform waved until the train disappeared in a cloud of smoke and steam.

Eleanor walked home beside her neighbour Millie. Neither woman spoke until they reached their houses.

"Fancy a cuppa Ellie?"

"Yeah, good idea. Thanks."

The women sat together in Millie's kitchen, cradling steaming cups of tea.

"Well, I think they'll be alright now, don't you. It's been a real worry lately with all this talk of bombing raids. It's a weight off, I tell you."

Eleanor took a sip and looked thoughtfully into the brown liquid without answering her friend.

"What d'you think Ellie?"

Eleanor looked up, her lips quivering as tears tumbled down her cheeks.

"Where are they going Millie? We don't know, do we?"

"You mustn't worry Ellie", empathised Millie. "They're in safe hands and they'll send us a postcard when they get where they're going. This war'll be over soon and they'll be back before you know it."

"I know, I'm just being silly." Eleanor wiped away her tears with the back of her hand.

"I'm just worried about Rob and I think I might have another little one on the way."

"Oh, that's lovely Ellie, congratulations! No wonder you're feeling a bit teary. Have you heard from your Rob since he was called up?"

"I got a letter last week, but I've no idea where he is. I've written to tell him that the kids have been evacuated, but God knows when he'll get that."

They sat drinking their tea in silence for a few moments, neither really feeling like chatting.

"Well, thanks for the tea Millie. I'd better be getting back now."

"Right you are love, keep your pecker up Ellie. Everything'll be alright."

Eleanor waited two long weeks for the postcard telling her that her children had been billeted in Lancashire. There wasn't much information on the postcard, but Eleanor read the childish scrawl over and over again, leaving it on her bedside table so she could read it last thing at night and first thing in the morning.

The young evacuees had spent all of that first day on trains and buses, being 'distributed' to various countryside villages. They were ushered into church and village halls, school rooms, and anywhere large enough to host the influx of tired little people needing somewhere safe to live, away from the predicted German invasion. Things had appeared to be well organised initially, but it became clear that there hadn't been enough homes arranged to take in all the evacuees. With some last minute crisis management, the 'leftovers' in many places were lined up cattle-market style and offered to townsfolk to choose who they liked the look of.

Jessica and Billy were picked out by two couples. It was a huge wrench for them both to realise that they would not be staying together. Jessica had to muster all her courage to honour her promise to her mother.

"Please, mister, can my brother come with me? I promised my mum I would look after him."

The adults had a short discussion, but it wasn't the answer she wanted.

"I'm sorry luv. We've only got room for one each. But you don't have to worry about your brother. You'll see him at school and can visit when you like."

So at the close of day, Jessica walked home with 'Uncle' Albert and 'Auntie' Pamela Pickering to the village butcher shop. Entering the spacious apartment above the shop, the couple gently explained how they liked to run their household. Jessica was pleasantly surprised to learn that she would be able to use a proper indoor bathroom with hot running water. It was a real novelty to prepare for bed in what she felt was luxury. Auntie Pam then showed the tired, nervous young girl into a room with a truckle bed, chest of drawers and wardrobe.

"Here you are me bonny. You'll be worn out, I'll bet, so just you get yourself into bed and try to get some sleep. We'll take you down to school in the morning. You'll probably see your brother as well. And you can write to your mam to let her know where you are. Sleep tight now."

Jessica smiled weakly. Maybe this wasn't going to be so bad, she thought as she climbed under the blankets.

Across the other side of the village, Billy was arriving at a small dairy farm, the home of the Ashton family. Ivy and Albert Ashton had three other children, John aged 4, Beryl, 8 and Freddie,11. They appeared fascinated by this newcomer who spoke with a funny accent. Billy did his best to answer the barrage of questions thrown at him by the other children, but eventually the adults recognised that the young Londoner was in desperate need of sleep.

"Right come on you lot, give the poor lad a break", announced Albert. "It's been a long day for this nipper, so I think it's time you all went up to bed. D'you agree mother?"

"Aye, I do. Come on kids." Ivy gathered her brood together, ushering them towards the stairs. "You'll have to top 'n' tail with our John, Billy. And I don't want to hear any of you messing about tonight, or there'll be trouble – right?"

"Don't you worry, mam, I'll keep 'em in line," promised Freddie in his big brother way.

"Good man, Fred." Albert ruffled his eldest son's hair as the children made their way past him to bed.

Just ten minutes later, the four tired, but excited children snuggled under the covers. There was some whispered questioning and stifled giggling for a while, until one by one they drifted off to sleep.

The following day saw the evacuees being introduced to the village school. They had to quickly become accustomed to the new way of doing things, making new friends, and dealing with name-calling in the playground. A few scuffles brought the wrath of teachers administering a smart clip round errant ears, and the command to shake hands and make friends. It would take a few weeks for the local children to accept the 'vaccies', as they became known. An uneasy truce gradually formed, but many of the children found friendship that made their upturned world more bearable.

Back in London, Eleanor was feeling queasy and the rocky bus journey wasn't helping her efforts to contain her stomach contents. Not a moment too soon, the red double-decker arrived outside the telephone exchange and she hurried into the Ladies before reporting for duty. With Rob somewhere in France, her children hundreds of miles away and now this, Eleanor felt her heart would break with the sadness and worry. She should have felt happy that she had been blessed with Rob's child, but right now, she was overwhelmed by the uncertainty of her situation. She took a deep breath and joined her colleagues.

"Mornin' Ellie. Blimey, you look rough. Still got that morning sickness, have you? That's lasted a long time, hasn't it?"

Eleanor sat in front of the switchboard panel.

"Yeah, this one's even worse than it was with the others." She pulled on her telephonist's headset and drew out the metal end of a cord to push into a socket corresponding to a flashing lamp. "Operator, which number do you require?" She spoke clearly and waited. "Thank you caller, putting you through."

"Have you seen the paper today?" Millie asked after she'd dealt with another caller.

"No, I was too busy trying not to throw up on the bus."

"They're calling this a 'phoney war', 'cos nothing's happened for a few months. So much for Operation Pied Piper taking our kids away to safety. Reg and I are talking about going to fetch ours back. We really miss 'em." A lamp lit up again on the switchboard. "Operator, which number?"

"What are you talking about?" Asked Eleanor when Millie had finished her call. "Can we do that?"

"Well who's going to stop us? They're our kids."

By the end of the day, Eleanor had resolved to travel to Lancashire and bring her children back to London. She handed her notice in and the next day was on the train travelling north, smiling uncontrollably at the thought of being reunited with her beautiful children.

Some hours later, a tired Eleanor walked into the butcher's shop as Albert Pickering was washing down the marble slabs.

"Sorry, luv I'm closing now …. oh, you're not from round here, are you? Can I help you?" As he asked the question, he thought the stranger looked slightly familiar.

"No, I'm Eleanor Franklin. I've come to see my kids."

"Aah, that explains it. She's the spit o' you." Albert smiled, wiped his hands on his apron and extended one to shake hers. "Lovely to meet you lass."

Eleanor sighed with relief. The first impression of the couple who had taken Jessica into their home for the last few months was reassuring. Pamela was also very welcoming, although with some reserve. She and Albert had not had any children and had become very fond of Jessica. The thought of her going back to her mother was a bit of a double-edged sword really, but they knew they should be happy for her.

Jessica was overjoyed to see her mother. The two of them hugged and cried without speaking for some minutes before being able to laugh at their display of emotion. Pamela looked on, shedding silent tears of her own, until Albert broke the spell.

"How about a brew then, Pam? We could probably all do with one, eh."

"Yes, sorry, forgetting me manners. I'll put kettle on." Pamela brushed her tears briskly away and retreated to the kitchen.

Eleanor was thankful for the tea, but keen to collect Billy without delay. Albert insisted on taking her and Jessica out to the Ashton's dairy farm in his delivery van. Billy's reunion with his mother was no less emotional than that of his sister's. He had got used to having 'brothers' to play with, but had missed his mother far more than he would admit.

The kindly northerners worried about Eleanor and the children going straight back to London, so between them they managed to find beds for the little family. The following morning, Eleanor thanked the foster parents again and promised to keep in touch with them as they said their farewells at the railway station.

Back in London Jessica and Billy were pleased to see their old friends again. Swapping accounts of good and bad experiences was commonplace, although those who had been unhappy in their billets preferred to forget their time away. Some found it difficult to adjust to life in the city again, especially those who had spent happy days enjoying the freedom to run across fields, climb trees and learn about farm and wild animals.

As the weeks went by, the war showed no sign of ending. The children were sent back to school, but many days were spent in the air raid shelters. Teachers did what they could to provide some education for the youngsters, but the odds were stacked against them. The children were destined to have a very different learning experience in the city.

One morning in Spring, Eleanor was manoeuvring her large midriff carefully around the oven door as she tried to clean the appliance without leaning in too far, when she heard a sharp knock on the front door. She struggled to her feet and waddled down the hallway as a second knock sounded.

"Alright, I'm coming", she called. "Bloomin' impatient", she muttered as she pulled open the door. When she saw who stood on the doorstep, Eleanor's mouth fell open and she felt faint.

"Rob! Oh, Rob you're home!"

"Well, aren't you going to let me in then?" he grinned as he stepped over the threshold and wrapped one arm around his wife. She noticed then that one of Rob's arms was held in a sling.

" Oh, you're injured. What happened?"

"Oh, just a bit of shrapnel. They sent me home to mend, so here I am me darlin'. And look at you – must be about ready to pop, I'd say."

"No, I've got another month to go, but I'll be glad when it's here. Oh Rob, I'm so glad to see you." They held each other as closely as Eleanor's middle would allow and kissed longingly.

"Are the kids here then?" They slowly pulled apart and Rob looked about him expecting the children to appear.

"No, silly, they're at school. Well, they spend more time down the shelters I think."

As Eleanor said her words, there came the long ominous wail of the siren, which seemed to haunt every day of the city dwellers' lives.

"I don't believe it", complained Eleanor. "When is this going to end? I'm fed up with going down those shelters day in day out. And half the time it's not even necessary."

"We could stay here if you want, luv", Rob suggested. "Like you say, it's probably not even going to come to anything."

"Alright. I'll put the kettle on for a cuppa. Those shelters are so hot and smelly; I don't think I can stomach it today. The kids'll be alright, won't they? Oh, they're going to be so pleased to see you when they get home."

Eleanor went into the kitchen, followed by her husband. She bent to close the oven door and felt a sudden searing pain that wrapped itself around her back and abdomen. She gasped and held her bump, her face showing the fear she felt. Rob was instantly worried, and helped his wife to a chair.

"You alright, luv? Can I get you anything?" Eleanor was about to speak, but another pain took her breath away as she leaned into her husband for comfort.

"I think you'd better go get the midwife Rob. Looks like there's someone else who's looking forward to seeing you!"

So the returning soldier raced down the street to find the midwife, but he could only find air raid wardens. He frantically searched the nearby shelters and eventually found the woman he was looking for. By that time, fear for his wife was making him feel physically sick.

The midwife reluctantly agreed to accompany Rob, but when they emerged from the underground sanctuary, it was evident that this time the siren had not been a false alarm. Rob felt a cold dread envelope him as he absorbed the devastation around him. He ran, stumbling through the streets until he came to his house. Or what used to be his house.

He clambered over the rubble desperately searching for a sign of life, but nothing had survived this onslaught. He fell to his knees, a broken man.

Minutes, or was it years later, Rob felt a hand on his shoulder. A gentle voice sympathised.

"Come on Rob, let's go. You've got two lovely children waiting for you down at the school. They're going to need you now."

The Gamble

'Well kids, if you're reading this then I'm gone.' The letter shook in Ann's hand.

'This is as far as I got before calling you', she said. Her eyes held the sparkle of unshed tears. Her hair, usually neatly tied back, showed signs of her distress.

'I thought I would wait. Actually I didn't want to be by myself.'

Susan, Genna, Gary and Kenneth sat on the chairs around the hexagon table in their mother's house. Four white envelopes stood propped up against the blue pebble vase. The house felt empty. No newspapers littered the glossy table top. The ashtray was bright and clean. From her place beside the table, Ann could see into the small kitchen, now neat and tidy. No pots sitting in readiness on the stove. The realisation that her mother had obviously spent some time cleaning and sorting things out added to her feelings of uncertainty.

'Keep reading Ann,' Kenneth said. 'I don't want to open mine.'

' "Whoa! Hang on!" No, that's not me. That's actually what mum has written', she looked across the table at Gary. He was grinning.

'That's mum. No grammar!' he laughed.

'Well, yes,…anyway. "Whoa! Hang on now no long faces! I didn't bring you up to be dippy Doras now did I? I know, I just put I'm gone", she read, "but I ain't dead; I'm just gone, as in I'm not here. Ann, I guess it's you that's doing the honours. I reckon you picked the letter up when you came to see me this morning. If that's right, then it's Tuesday. Then you got on the jungle drums and called the others. Am I right?"

Ann nodded. Kenneth was pulling at his short beard. Susan smiled at Gary.

'Mum's right as usual', she said. 'We always did think she was a witch.'

'Yeah…remember when we searched the back of her head?', Gary reminded them, 'we were sure she had eyes there!'

Gary stood at the window and stood looking out at the small garden.

'Grass needs cutting', he said.

'I'll make us a cup of tea, shall I?' Susan asked. She went into the kitchen glad of something to do. Ann was talking as if something tragic had happened. Susan crossed her fingers as she got the cups from the cupboard. The kettle had been given a polish along with the rest of the kitchen. Susan smiled; she knew her mum hated housework. It must have taken supreme effort on her part to leave everything so clean.

'Anyway, shall I read the rest? Or do you want to open your own envelopes?'

'Carry on Ann', Kenneth nodded at her.

"You remember that over 60s trip I went on last year? Last year March it was. The one you together said would be too much for me, would tire me out, and use all my savings up. We went right up to Foxton Locks, right up there in Northampton. Oh it were grand! I sat by that canal thinking what a lovely life it would be, drifting along as a barge person. I fancied the gypsy life, you know."

'Oh mum!' Susan said, 'what have you gone and done now?'

Gary was laughing. 'She's probably run away with the gypsies!' he laughed, 'that would be just like mum. Remember when she bought her car?' he laughed louder. 'Oh my goodness Kenny, you should have seen your face, your beard nearly tripped you up so low did your chin fall!'

'Yes, well I was a little surprised at her choice, I must say. A 1959 pink Cadillac is hardly the thing you expect to see your elderly mother driving round the streets in.'

'Well at least she sold that motorbike', Gary said, 'coulda been worse – she always fancied a Brough Superior, not that a little old thing like her would ever have been able to start it!'

'It wouldn't a stopped her trying. Carry on Ann', Kenneth said, 'before Gary has us believing mother has sold herself to the Arabs.'

67

'Anyway', Ann continued, "you know old Martin Morris? Him that sniffs and wipes his nose on his cuff, well he sat alongside of me, sniffing a bit and chatting. We talked a lot about drifting through life and all that. Well he ain't ever been married or had kids, or a car. Well anyways, he start to come round here a few evenings a week for a cuppa. We kept on talking about selling up and moving to somewheres hot. I thought it was all talk, but I got me a passport; just in case. He's good company is old Martin, well, when he ain't sniffing. Well, last month he says to me, "Pack yer bags girl; I've just been and gone and bought us a villa thing in Monte Carlo. Now that's the gambler's paradise, so take a gamble." That's what he said! So that's what I've done. He were right serious, so I took the gamble and that's where I am right now, sunning me old bones and adding a few more wrinkles to me collection."

Ann looked up from reading. Susan and Gary sat touching their envelopes. Kenneth walked round the room, touching the pictures that hung on the wall, running his hand over the highly polished sideboard.

'Why didn't she mention all this before?' Genna asked. 'I mean it seems a huge thing to do at her age, and how do we know that Mr Morris hasn't taken all her savings and will send her home penniless?'

'She actually answers that question, right here in the letter,' Ann said. 'Listen, "why didn't I tell you before? Well what would you together have said; it would've been *oh mum, at your age!* Or *oh mum, what about your bad knees,* so I didn't tells you."

"Kenny, in your letter you'll find the keys to the house. Gen, you've got the deeds, Gary, you've got the keys to me car and Susan, you've got the job of selling the lot and sharing it out. I give you the job 'cos you were always the fairest. Ann, cheer up girl, no more Tuesday duty visits for you!"

"Now I tried me best for all of you, and if I failed, well then I'm sorry. But you haven't turned out a bad bunch, all honest and hard working. I'm laughing as I write this bit, yes, even you Gary, but you were a little bugger, you'd take anything that weren't nailed down! Kenny you always looked after us; you were the man after your father went. Trailing after that scrag-end of a blonde he ended up with. Still, he is your dad."

"You're all adults now, with your own lives. Gen, you're the babe and you're forty now. Kenny, you're past the half way mark. So sell up and have fun with the money. I've took all me sentimental bits, so anything you want to keep, well keep it, other than sell that is. That vase on the table, well that's a Clarence Cliff (I think that's how you spell it) so it should be worth a few bob. I ain't going to tell you what you already know. Kenny, you know how them auction places work, Gary, you watch all them 'flog it' programmes so you won't be fiddled. If you find the time or find yourself down St Tropez way, well you can always call in on me and Sniffy. He don't sniff so much now, and as for wiping his nose on his shirt sleeve? Well he'd have a job; he only wears t-shirts now.

I love you all, so take care and wish me well.

From mum, PS My address is: Grimaud 63, St Tropez.

PPS Martin decided that Monte Carlo was a little too noisy, but it ain't far away. You should see our house, well it's a blinking mansion compared to the one you're standing in now. I'll need a motor bike to get me from the front room to the lav!

When you do come, bring the kids and your swim suit…we've only got our own pool ain't we! Now how posh is *that*?
Oh, and before I forget, can you all try and get March the 20th off work. I'm only asking because I would like you all, yep, that means all the kids as well, (Martin say don't worry about the cost, 'cos he'll

69

see to it; I would like you all to be here, the reason being that as it's the anniversary of us going to Foxton Locks and well, when we kind of started, well I suppose you could say 'dating'.

Martin has booked that date for us to go and get married. What a turn up hey! Your old mum flirting with a millionaire and I didn't even know."

By Sandy

www.ingramcontent.com/pod-product-compliance
Lightning Source LLC
Chambersburg PA
CBHW071205130626
46555CB00004B/1589